DRACULA
THE UNTOLD STORY

and

DRACULA
ON A GHOST TRAIL

Rex Greenwood
Ann Brady

Pen & Ink Designs

In Loving Memory of a wonderful Father,
Grandfather and Uncle,
as well as a humorous human being who
brought much fun and joy to many people.

Gone but not forgotten – your legacy lives on.
We miss you very much.

The Cystic Fibrosis Trust

All royalties generated from the sale of this
book are to be donated to the Cystic Fibrosis
Trust in the name of Rex Greenwood.

This was a charity very close to Rex's
heart and one he supported by playing his
characters of Count Dracula
and Captain Cook.

If you have bought this book,
we thank you for your donation.

CONTENTS

FOREWORD BY ANN BRADY   I

INTRODUCTION BY REX GREENWOOD   IV

DRACULA - THE UNTOLD STORY

CHAPTER 1   1

CHAPTER 2   7

CHAPTER 3   12

CHAPTER 4   19

CHAPTER 5   24

DRACULA ON A GHOST TRAIL

CHAPTER 1   30

CHAPTER 2   37

CHAPTER 3   45

CHAPTER 4   53

CHAPTER 5   58

CHAPTER 6   64

CHAPTER 7   70

ENTERTAINER WHO WAS AMBASSADOR

FOR TOWN   74

FOREWORD

BY ANN BRADY

Rex Greenwood was my uncle, a younger brother of my father and one of five children born in South Yorkshire. He had a brilliant sense of humour, a memory which has stayed with me all my life. I spent many a summer holiday in his and my cousins' company where we played great games and laughed a lot.

His portrayal of Dracula, Captain Cook, and the Whitby Town Crier gave a lot of pleasure, and benefitted many people through his charitable work. Sometimes even scaring a few. But in a nice way.

Uncle Rex often told me stories about his adventures when portraying Dracula. About how he used to hide near the old Whitby Abbey and wait for the school children and other visitors to arrive. He was to show them around and tell them his stories. Upon arrival he would jump out of hiding, causing much laughter.

His visit 'down under' at the request of the Australian Government was as part of the celebrations for the Centenary of the country's Founding Father Captain Cook who himself hailed from Whitby. Rex was also asked by the Australian Health Department to dress as Dracula to promote the use of garlic as a health food and to give blood. Both he and my Aunt had a wonderful time.

There were also many other interviews and one which has always stuck in my mind was by an American journalist researching the history of Dracula. She had been travelling through Transylvania and other countries, before finally arriving in Whitby where Bram Stoker had written his story. Taking her for coffee at a local café the lady began questioning Rex about his belief in Dracula. The conversation went something like this:

Lady: "Of course, you don't really believe in the character, do you?"

Before he could answer the coffee was brought to the table and as the lady was distracted Rex, having had some special Dracula teeth made, took the opportunity to change his own teeth for these. Then, taking hold of the lady's hand he slowly turned it palm up as she repeated the question.

Smiling, Rex responded by showing his teeth and saying, "But of course I do my dear!" Whereupon, he moved as if to bite her wrist.

The desired effect was created, and the lady screamed, "You do, you do."

The lady who owned the café, coming to see

what had happened, sighed and promptly scolded Rex for misbehaving.

Such was his great sense of humour.

Sadly, my Uncle lost his battle with cancer in 2004 and is sorely missed by all our family and friends alike. I have decided, with my cousins' agreement, to reissue these two stories, written by my Uncle, in order to continue his wonderful memory and legacy.

Ann Brady
Co-author

Remember: Whether you believe in the legend of Dracula or not is down to you. These stories were written by someone with a deep sense of humour. He enjoyed playing a character which, over the years, brought pleasure to many, as well as himself. I hope you enjoy reading his take on the 'Count'.

INTRODUCTION

BY REX GREENWOOD

Born in Thurnscoe, Yorkshire on 4th March 1926, and weighing in at around 1¾ lbs, I could not walk or talk until I was five years old. Needless to say, I made up for it afterwards! Old friends of my parents, George and Eddy Easton, who were at the time entertainers on the stage in-between making silent movies, gave me Bram Stokers biography book and so it all began.

Having something in common with Bram Stoker, a very weak infancy, I felt an affinity towards him. Thus, a strange friendship began with a person I had never met. Yet, one to whom I felt uncannily close. In fact, close to both him and his 'Count Dracula'. It was this 'relationship' that changed my life. I suppose, in a way, due to the fact that I could live out my fantasies through the Count.

I distinctly remember a friend taking me to Sunderland in 1933 to see Bela Lugosi. And, although

I was only seven, his performance left a profound impression on the then young boy. Ludlam's 'Biography of Bram Stoker' has been my 'Bible' and enabled me to act out my 'other life.' The 'Dracula' in me has I suppose, brought me a form of fame, while enabling me to help others. My father had a saying... "One crowded hour of glorious fame is worth an age without a name!" I am very fortunate to have had many such hours.

As I grew older, I eventually became an MC in and around the Doncaster area, with Dracula being part of my act. A varied and interesting career, followed by a move to Whitby led to my becoming their Town Crier for nine years. Together with Dracula and Captain Cook, this gave me a tremendous amount of happiness. And, I am glad to say, brought much pleasure and assistance to a lot of local charities. All my funds went to the local branch of the Friends of Cystic Fibrosis.

Trips to Europe and Australia, with my characters, together with TV appearances mean I have experienced a very full and rewarding life. With the finest character, of course, being "Dracula".

Whitby accepted me as a son of the town, along with my characters and, shall we say, my slightly different views. But, probably primarily due to my work as the Town Crier. I received a lot of help from all kinds of people, including my photographer friend Alan Wastell and the staff from Whitby Pavilion. This support at no time being more apparent than when I underwent surgery for cancer in my thyroid.

The people of Whitby were magnificent. There were so many good wishes and such faith. Yes, faith! I worked very well alongside our vicar, Rev. Ben Hopkinson, never going into the churchyard or the likes of that. Needless to say, the surgery put paid to the Town Crying, leaving me to concentrate on my other characters.

I believe 'Dracula' should be a fun thing for all, and something to be used for the good of the people and to help others. I feel this is what Bram Stoker would have liked and wanted. I believe if he were to know how distorted his story has become in the films, through societies etc., he would probably come back as 'Dracula' himself and haunt us all!

Still, I suppose no-one really knows. Except perhaps I, Count Rex Dracula. I know, and I am not telling...

Yours

Count Rex Dracula
Circa 1985

Dracula

The Untold Story

CHAPTER 1

The thin line between fact, fiction, fantasy and imagination can be slim indeed. Especially, when a person wants to believe something is real. No-one is more aware of this than I. Nor readier to admit that somewhere deep, deep within our minds lurks the reality of another existence. Another world which straddles both past and present. A life some would call fantasy, but which others might shy away from. Even fear!

Many things have been written of Bram Stoker's 'Dracula,' and no doubt, much more is still to follow. As I don my Dracula outfit to attend some local function, I feel strongly the part I am about to play. Why don't you come with me now into that twilight world? The one that is both past and present at the same time. Another dimension where fantasy becomes confused with fact, and fiction fuses with the present.

You may feel, as I do the dread of the mighty sea. So much so that I will not swim in it. Feel also Dracula's dread of the ocean and his fear of the journey to England as he (or is it I?) am tossed around in the flimsy wooden boat.

I feel myself, rather than him, being watched by the blood-red eyes of the ship's dog. Always alert for signs of panic. But I too feel the hidden fear of the greatness of the sea and the sudden lurch as we are washed into it.

Time passes. A vague awareness of the red eyes of the dog overpowers me as he comes closer. Ever closer and more menacing. The feeling (though not the pain) as he sinks his teeth into my neck. Then again that dreamlike state as a sense of deep sleep sweeps over me!

Am I really on that sandy shore, feeling the small waves lapping at my clothes? Rolling me gently, ever onwards towards the shadow of the red-eyed dog who eventually stands over me, like a four-legged seminal.

For yes, he is red-eyed still, but no longer alert. No longer leering. Somehow, he looks more contented. There is a more pleasing look evident on his face. He glances once more at my wave-sodden form, as if to check I am now able to fend for myself. Then he is off. Bounding across the sands, he eventually vanishes into the early dawn mist, away on his journey to a place I know not. But where, if fate decrees, I shall subsequently discover it.

I fight the long battle against sleep. Do I want to sleep? Have I slept? I cannot really tell. All I know is that I must not sleep here. A force, alien to my nature, drives me towards Whitby's 199 steps and the cliff-top graveyard which is to be found at the steps summit. The force urges me to seek out some small plot of unhallowed ground, leading my footsteps to the sandstone tombstones. They are marked only with skull and crossbones, indicating the final resting places of the pirates.

What next?

As my muddled mind fights to cast off the overpowering feeling of sleep, a voice pierces my oblivion like a wooden stake.

"Hi there, Sir... Could you direct me to the grave of Dracula, Buddy?"

I turn, a little startled, seeing the face of a smiling American tourist. He repeats the question. "Dracula's grave, Buddy. It's around here somewhere, isn't it?"

My mind is now composed. I am alert, awake, self-assured. I look him straight in the eye and tell him, "You couldn't be nearer, Sir, for the grave is here, and I am he."

The American stands still. An amazed expression crosses his face. He is nervous and slightly confused, but slowly a wide grin crosses his face. "Say, fella, that's rich." He looks towards his female companion. "Ha, hear that Mabal? This guy's Dracula."

We chat amicably about Whitby and its legends. About its stories, both fact and fiction, before parting cheerily with a friendly wave. Only I, it seems, was aware of the black dog with the red eyes who sat watching us during our conversation. And who glared at the American stranger, seeking the look of panic in his eyes.

Was the dog real, or imagined? Is playing the part of Dracula going to my head?

"Follow me now down the 199 steps," I hear the dog say! "Wait with me as I pause to look for the wreck of a ship."

Then I realise that as real as it might have seemed, it was only a figment of my imagination. There is no wreck down there.

I reach the bottom of the 199 steps. Let me check once more to see if there is a wreck on the beach below for I am still unsure if the thought was pure imagination. The smell of oak-smoked kippers fills the air as I pass the smokehouse. A black dog almost trips me as I wend my way up Henrietta Street. "Go home dog and find your master," I snarl.

As I walk along, I start to feel my true self. I see the smiling face of my old friend Bob, coming towards me. Bob, is quite a character. Well known to members of the town's Regatta committee, and others within the area.

"Morning, Bob."

"Morning, Rex. Seen anything of your old pal, Dracula up there?"

I smile, he will have his little joke. The fool, doesn't realise that one day I will bite his neck?

The dog follows. I throw a stone at him. But he will not be diverted from pursuing me. He follows, just as he did of old when smiling fisher-lasses trod these cobbled streets. Going about their daily business, never realising who I was, who I am, who... Oh! I am so confused.

In my confusion I once more face the town, my head is buzzing. Why am I up Henrietta Street? I retrace my steps past Whitby's narrow passages, yards and quaint corners. All the places that can tell a thousand stories. Those that carry strange names, like Arguments Yard, which adds an air of interest and mystery to this fine old fishing town.

I am now crossing the old swing bridge. I pass the old fountain at the end, where top-hatted gentlemen step down from their horse-drawn carriages to drink. Strange that this should be for the fountain has not worked in many years.

Passing street urchins and flower sellers along St. Anne's Staith I wend my way towards Khyber Pass. There I come upon the house where Mina and Lucy stay... or stayed, for I am unsure where or when I am. I do not tarry for the building has unpleasant feelings, even for me.

As my mind clears, I move on to the West Cliff Hotel, built by Hudson the railway king and later owned by Rex Greenwood... Oh! Of course, I mean by me. That place holds many memories too. It's where I felt equally at home both as myself and as Dracula. But the building is not without its strange happenings. Many a time I remember laying the breakfast silver in the basement dining room, only to find it was gone the following morning. Some may suggest pilfering guests however, often by washing-up time, all the disappearing cutlery would have mysteriously come to light?

CHAPTER 2

It is evening now. I think back to Mina and Lucy, and the strange happenings which befell them. Where are they now? Did those things really happen to them or were they figments of the imagination? A conjuring up of strange creatures from the depths of the brain?

We all, at some time, will feel or see strange apparitions. Mine are with me now as I make my way along Crescent Avenue and into Royal Crescent. As I pass number 6, that fateful house, dusk suddenly falls. An eerie, orange glow emanates from the cliff tops, as the sun sets silently into the sea.

I am once more aware of those red eyes watching me. Looking around, I squint my own eyes, searching the gloom for the outline of the black dog. Sure enough, there within Crescent Gardens is a black shadow, watching. Following my every movement.

Turning I fight the compulsion to approach the dog. Bats skim my head, and just as quickly as they appeared, they disappear. Flying around the houses in

Church Square, before finally vanishing from whence they came.

I too must disappear. Back into the world of reality. Back to my guests waiting to be served their evening meal at the West Cliff Hotel. But wait... is this too not so? Does it belong to another reality? Another time, from long gone.

But no, I know it is now for I am serving evening meals. "Good evening everyone, what a beautiful night for a steak." Momentarily my blood runs cold. Why do I think of a wooden stake, when I say that?"

My mind slips again into that old feeling. My teeth ache. The fangs seem to want to stretch down. I lick my lips for they are dry. My eyes appear to overflow with a red mist, but... no, no... NO, NO, NO. The time is not right.

I engage my guests in conversation as a diversion to the thoughts now entering my mind. They must not sense what is happening. The conversation turns to the performances of Bella Lugosi, Christopher Lee and Louis Jordan. My guests are telling me how watching these actors makes them believe. How it awakens their minds to the reality of the characters.

Do they know? I cannot risk it. I must leave immediately before my conversation or appearance gives me away.

The mist outside feels cool and refreshing. I

stand on the small hill known locally as 'Spion Kop'. Glancing down into the dark hollow of Khyber Pass my eyes pass towards the shadow of the imposing building known as 'Streanaeshalch'. The architecture of the building is almost castle-like, lending a strange air of mystery to this part of town. No wonder at one time, it was said to be so haunted it remained empty for many years.

I take a seat, and my mind transforms the building into Dracula's Castle. Strange, for at this very moment I am rubbing my fingers subconsciously over a plaque attached to the seat. One which commemorates Bram Stoker.

The feeling is there again. All things seem to fit. Is it a coincidence that this seat should be so marked, being close to Streanaeshalch, and Royal Crescent? As well as being within sight of both Tate Hill Sands, the church and the abbey. Is it a coincidence that it is I who sits here on this chilly evening? Teeth aching, eyes misty and a brain full of the thoughts of Dracula? No, my friends, it is not coincidence, for fate is with me.

A man approaches, and without being told, I know it is Dracula he seeks. Little does he realise how close he has come to the object of his quest.

"Excuse me," he asks, confidently. "Are you a local? Can you tell me about Dracula?"

I point out the abbey and the steps, telling him the story of Bram Stoker's Dracula. I explain the town's connections with the story before allowing him to turn and leave. I know this is the time. I believe. The teeth begin to ache once more, and I feel the pressure of growth in my fangs. As he turns away, I lean forward, fangs poised!

"I say, did you see that black dog climbing the 199 steps? I am sure he just came off Tate Hill Sands? Just like the one in the Dracula story eh? Gives you the creeps doesn't it?"

Foiled again. Am I to be forever haunted by that blasted dog?

I retract my fangs. The moment has gone. Pleasant conversation must be made to cover my true identity. "Nothing unusual in that Sir. There's quite a lot of that type of dog in Whitby." I point to the houses above us at Crescent Place. "Did you know that is where the solicitor's house was?"

"Oh, how interesting," he says, before bidding me good night. He will be mine. Later.

The darkness is now more welcoming than ever, yet I am feeling drawn towards the light of a nearby public house. What strange power is pulling me in I do not know but go I must. Forwards to the alien lights of the public bar.

As I enter the tavern, the modern electric lights are gone. Candle smoke fills the air. Wine-sodden sailors sit around talking noisily. A mixture of fish, tar and ale fills my nostrils. I order a mug of porter.

"A pint Sir? Certainly," says the barman.

A friend beckons me from across the room. "I've just ordered a steak Rex; will you have one with me?"

I genuinely shudder. "Don't talk to me about stakes; they make me go cold!"

My friend laughs but still he orders another steak for me anyway.

"How would you like it?" asks the waitress.

"Rare," I reply. "Very, very rare... "

Later, once well satisfied on Porter and Steak, we leave the tavern. I drop back a little as my friend trundles unsteadily along the cobbled quayside, singing to himself. Again, the time is right. I stop as my fangs begin to grow, wait as my red-misted eyes clear slightly, and then... I go for the neck...

A scream echoes around the empty street. My friend falls to the ground in front of me, cowering before the jaws of a large black dog. It is sinking its teeth into the man's neck, then his ankles, his arms, until finally its bloodlust is satiated.

I scream. "Curse you dog, he was to be mine. You knew this. He was to be mine."

I hear a loud whistle! The peelers are coming. Quickly, the dog slinks away, blood dripping from its fangs. I too slip into the shadows, going along the crag until I fall exhausted, the sound of ambulance sirens ringing in my ears.

CHAPTER 3

Today is another day. I walk jauntily down Flowergate, into Golden Lion Bank and onto Bridge End where all the local fishermen are gathered, chatting. This morning's conversation is centred around an incident on Pier Road the previous evening. It appears some poor chap came out of the pub drunk and was knocked down by a hit-and-run driver. Strangely, his injured body was then set upon by some savage dogs. Or so it would seem?

Taking the bridge to the east side, the real Whitby in many people's eyes, I am drawn once more up the 199 grey-stone steps to the graveyard above. The sun shines down pleasantly as a figure in a dog-collar approaches. I recognise him as the new vicar. He is apparently looking for something.

"Searching for Dracula's grave?" I ask with a smile.

"Oh, good morning Mr Greenwood. No indeed, don't mention such things, they are better left alone. I am looking for something though. It's a large black dog which was making a nuisance of itself by howling during bell-ringing last night. Someone told me they've just seen it come up the steps."

Is it true? Has that accursed dog followed me again? Indeed, I saw no dog as I climbed the steps alone this morning.

The vicar leaves, searching relentlessly behind each tombstone. I continue on towards the pirates' gravestones, where tell-tale drips of blood stain the stone pavement in front of them. The dog has been here. But where is it now?

When will this nightmare end, for one day it surely must?

Glancing over the wall, I look beyond the abbey with its awe-inspiring spectral shadows. Contrasting with the grey-stone walls they glint in the sunshine. Momentarily my eyes turn back, before instantly returning towards the abbey, whose image has not had time to leave my retina. Sure enough, there perched high up on the old stone ruins is the black, red-eyed dog. How he got there I know not. But there he is. His fearless eyes scan mine for signs of panic. But no, I am less fearful of him now.

One day I am determined I shall be his master. One day he shall fear me.

My mind is calmer now. I drift through the passages of time, imagining the characters of old standing before me. Caedmon, St. Hilda, pirates by the dozen, fishermen and pallbearers, farm lasses and gentlefolk. All have found their final resting place in this land of tombs. One day I too may rest here. But not before I have become master of that menacing dog, which even now watches me from up on high, within the abbey ruins. Watches me as I make my way towards the modern TV mast on the Abbey Plain.

I divert momentarily to look over the cliff edge, down into the harbour and river with its modern yachts. And in doing so remember the fateful day I arrived here. When that accursed dog stood over me on the wet sand. The feeling comes again as I fight the red mist which threatens to fill my eyes.

Visions of tall sailing ships alternate with modern craft. I look astonished at the pier extensions which suddenly disappear and then reappear as my mind switches between times past and the present. Drawing away from the cliffs the mist fades. Now I must walk and clear my head. Yes, I must walk. Walk in order to fight the inner self. To battle the curse which has befallen my soul since my arrival on the beach, when the red-eyed dog bit me.

I follow the route down Green Lane, past the end of the ropery and on towards Helredale, or Gallows Close as the locals call it. What is this I see? A new bridge crosses the Strange. I don't remember that, though it must be seven or eight years old now. Joining east side to the west. In much the same way as my mind appears to be able to bridge the past to the present. Fact to fiction. Truth to fantasy.

Moving over the bridge, I follow the road round towards Prospect Hill and descend Downdinner Hill. In Whitby, you can only drive up Downdinner Hill. I pass Hanover Terrace, a row of houses with a happy atmosphere despite the hauntings which are said to have taken place there. No. 10 I believe is of particular interest?

Come with me as I enter Pannett Park. Sit with me near the museum while I rest and gather my thoughts. Looking down upon Station Square I see the new hospital, the police station and the library. Would Bram Stoker approve of modern Whitby? I am not so sure he would.

Aware, perhaps by some sixth sense, I know someone is approaching. Someone who will once more ask those accursed questions which will bring the red mist to my eyes. And bring forward the character from inside which I cannot control.

I smile at the two lovely young things. "Would you mind if we sit with you and ask a few questions concerning Whitby?" Knowing what is to come, I hesitate, but finally consent to converse with the young ladies.

"Did Dracula really come from Whitby? Did he really exist?" The 'did he this, did he that,' continues. The same old questions unfolding but which I gladly give the answers to. Yet, with caution, for I know I cannot fight the deep conviction within me. The compulsion I have, where I am already considering the fresh young blood of my next victims.

"Is it true there is it to be a waxworks exhibition of the Dracula story on Whitby's seafront?"

This is something I cannot answer. Can this be true that his, no... my image is to be cast in wax for public viewing?

I am the one now eagerly asking questions. "Where is it to be?"

"Marine Parade."

"How do you know?"

"We read it in the 'Whitby Gazette' and the 'Northern Echo.' Also, the Town Crier has been telling people about it."

The Town Crier! Of course! But wait... that is me. I am once more confused, so quickly change the subject back to Pannett Park and its benefactor, Alderman Pannett who gave it to the town.

My eyes are taking in the smooth pale skin of their necks. The faint blue traces of the underlying veins. "Are you locals or day-trippers, ladies?" I ask.

"Oh, we are here on a fortnight's holiday."

"And may I be so bold as to ask your names?"

"Lucy and Minnie," one of them volunteers. "Well, Lucy and Mina really, but I don't like Mina, it's such an unusual, old-fashioned name."

LUCY?... LYNDA?... MINA?... MANDY?... Similar to my daughter's names. What strange trick is fate playing on me? Am I forever to be cursed with signposts to my other self?

I am shaken now but manage a smile as I continue to tell them the tales of Whitby. Of how the lily pond in the park is now a shadow of its former glory. And how, within a short stroll, one can see what is reputedly the oldest inhabited house in Whitby, Bagdale Old Hall. The hall once stood on the edge of Bagdale Beck, a small stream which runs into the harbour. It is still there but is covered by a road. Close to the hall was Bagdale Bridge a small crossing over the stream, but now the site of stepping stones.

I tell them about the hall and how it is supposed to be haunted by a noble gent. Apparently, he was a double agent, spying for both the Roundheads and the Cavaliers. He was also very friendly with the maid and taking his leave of her he went to support the Cavaliers. Unfortunately, the Roundheads took the hall in his absence. Upon his return he found the maid dead. He too was murdered, and since that time the pair are said to haunt the hall; walking its passages looking for each other.

I see a look of fear in one of the girls' eyes. Did I give the game away when I smiled, showing the increasing length of my teeth? They want to go, but I ask them to stay, stretching out my hand, trying to restrain Mina. I am trying to attain a position where I can reach their necks and drink, as I did of old, their fresh, young blood.

They seem more frightened now. Perhaps, they sense the danger. Suddenly getting up, they run away through the bushes towards Bagdale.

A scream suddenly fills the air, followed by another. I look but see nothing save for the tail of a black dog disappearing from view. And though I cannot see them, I know the dog with red eyes, has once again beaten me to my prey.

CHAPTER 4

Will I ever beat that ungodly dog? I know I must. Though I don't know how. Yet, I know fate decrees it shall be so. An idea begins to develop in my mind. Thank you, Trevor of York, for little do you know it, but you have become my saviour!

Once again dusk casts its shroud over us. On the dark horizon, Whitby Abbey stands in silhouette alongside St. Mary's Church. It casts a feeling of majesty to an otherwise dreary scene. The night envelopes Whitby's stately buildings, carved in many cases from locally quarried stone by local craftsmen. Houses which have seen the lifelines of many famous people. Such as Cook, Scoresby and Lascelles. As well as other less well known but equal in status in the eyes of many. Such as sailors, lifeboat coxswains and lords. Lord Normanby's Castle is also close by. Even tradesmen of all types have, and do live within the walls of Whitby's noble houses.

More are yet to be made famous, but soon another will become as famous... DRACULA.

They will remember me, if only because they wish to believe in me, for I am real if they think it so. I was lucky, yes lucky Mr Dog. Mr Black Dog with the red eyes, for you have released me from myself. I... We... are here to stay and come the dawn I will find a way to win, to conquer. To release myself finally from the bonds of my mind.

This morning there is much activity. My mind is clear, and I can traverse the chasms of impossibility. I do not see the two young ladies of yesterday, but I know they have woken from their sleep unsure of something. They are perhaps confused without knowing why. I sense their ill feelings. Neither will remember or care about the teeth marks left on their necks. Bit by the same dog I was while I was on that wave swept beach. They may not remember, but I will.

The streets of Whitby beckon me once more. I pass Hinton's supermarket, closed this Sunday morning. Moving down Golden Lion Bank, I find myself once more at the old fountain on the west end of Whitby Bridge. Today it seems different, as if in a different time? No top-hatted gentlemen stopping for a drink. No horse-drawn carriages clattering by, no water gushing from the fountain-head.

Today is a day of rest, so they say. If only I

could rest! But I shall never rest as long as these feelings keep welling up inside me. Just as they do now. My teeth feel uncomfortable. The high ones have reached a permanent, larger size, giving my face an unusual leer. Not unlike that which is evident on the face of the black dog. He will not survive, I am determined. It is only I who will survive. I who will go down in history. Who will remain in the corners of your memory, long after I have gone from your conscious mind.

The Harbourside is quiet as I pass Doran's photographic shop. I stop, transfixed by my reflection in the window. My teeth are genuinely long and prominent now. I will not be able to hide the truth for much longer.

The proprietor is inside. "Good Morning Mr Doran."

He smiles, returning my greeting. I enter the shop, consciously taking note of the layout of the premises. After browsing a short time, I make my excuses and leave. I head towards the fish quay with its rows of fishing boats and cobbles moored nearby. I still feel uneasy close to water, as well I might.

Prancing playfully on Tate Hill Sands is my red-eyed adversary, mixing unobtrusively with the children. His eyes, even at this distance, still follow my every move. He must not know the plan I have in mind. He must not suspect until it is too late, for eternity is at stake. At least for one of us. For the other, there is only death. And I am determined it shall be I who lives on.

Time passes, but my constant watch of the dog does not fail. He too watches me, yet I pray he has not perceived my change of mental attitude. Occasionally he seems to relax. At times diverting his ever-watching eyes from me, as if ready to join in to play with the local children. He jumps from Tate Hill Pier onto the sand, then back up onto the Pier, only to drop once more, almost playfully into the water.

I feel only disgust for this unearthly creature which has changed my life. Oh, I am thankful for the chance at immortality, which his bite has brought me. But, despite this thankfulness, I have an intense disgust and anger at the way he has toyed with me. Leading me towards the blood I now so eagerly crave only, on each occasion, to steal it from me at the last minute.

The way he manipulated fate to bring Lucy and Mina into my life. The way he used them to humiliate me. However, it shall be no more. I can wait. Wait until the time is right, and then, only then, will I take the final victory.

The dog plays with the children, but I see his mannerisms have changed. Now he waits by the water's edge, watching as the children dive into the water. Their playful screams having aroused his interest. He sits watching, waiting for a sign of panic which will trigger his senses. I know he will not wait much longer. As I watch, I see he is ready to create panic. Concentrating on one small boy in particular. And, as he watches, I watch him for I know he is now not watching me. My moment is nigh.

The boy screams as the dog grabs his arm. In the tumult that follows there is much activity as the adults beat at the dog with sticks, towels and other objects. I climb down onto a nearby fishing boat, quickly unclipping the distress flare and launch it towards the beach. The dog squeals in pain as the rocket pierces his side. Burning red hot smoke streams from his black body. He drops the child, unharmed, as his unearthly howl fills the air. No earthly creature could utter such a cry as that which comes from the animal.

As boat oars and other weapons rain down upon him, he looks for a means of escape. Glancing across the harbour he sees me, his only ally, and runs along Tate Hill Pier. He is intent on quenching the burning wound in the harbour water. Running towards me he dives, his four feet hitting the water together, hoping above hope that the underlying mud will not deter his escape.

Then suddenly it happens, for the mud holds more than his alert mind could have imagined. Far below the water's surface are the remains of the old wooden jetties, once used to tie up sailing craft. It was on one of these that fate decided he should die. I could not have predicted a more fitting end for the unearthly creature. He dies, impaled on a piece of wood. The old broken mooring has been my salvation, for he has perished with a stake through the heart.

CHAPTER 5

Now the story of the black dog has come to a conclusive end, my task of achieving immortality has become easier, though there is much work still to do.

It is a week since that day, and I am at home, my wife is talking on the telephone to Trevor.

"Where will they be stored?" I later ask, referring to the items they had been discussing. The answer is interesting as it fits in precisely with my plans.

I must act quickly and without raising any suspicions. Fate follows me, for it is my lifeblood and it dictates what I must do for soon I shall be dining at the Royal Hotel. It was itself once used by Bram Stoker in his day. But I shall be surrounded by those who will assist me in my quest for immortality?

We have dined, we have discussed my idea and it is to be. For now I bid farewell to the luncheon party and leave the hotel. I follow the promenade towards the turreted towers of that other building which was also formerly a large hotel, The Metropole. I continue past the Parade, on Upgang Lane to White Point Bridge and on towards Ruswarp, before returning to Whitby, full of fresh thoughts.

Soon the day arrives. The objects which my wife Gwen discussed on the phone, are being taken out of storage. Now I am ready, having spent the previous night completing my plan. It has not been difficult to cover myself in wax. Tomorrow, I shall be in the perfect position, having replaced myself as the waxwork dummy of Dracula. There in the museum, converted from Doran's photographic shop, I shall rest forever in peace.

What a plan, a brilliant idea. This way, I shall have the freedom of the night, and the pleasure of the day. And, in this modern age of moving figures and life-like models, who will suspect me. A sign will dare visitors to put their fingers into my mouth? And, at intervals, my mouth will close.

You see the plans which I, as Rex Greenwood, put to the dinner guests had all been carefully thought out for this very moment. Despite the audacity of the idea, I am still here. And I am ready to taste the salt blood of the first finger. Of that first daring visitor.

Dracula will never need leave Whitby again, for I now have all I need in this, my new resting place. Feasting any day, I choose. The public, I am sure will not mind, for I shall not be greedy.

However, for now, I shall sleep. But rest

assured I will be waiting here for you. Always in Whitby, beneath my wax cocoon, where I will live, and breathe.

Know I am waiting.

Ever ready for my first contact with YOU... Come and visit me... if you dare!!!

Dracula

on a
Ghost Trail

A tour of some of the ghost stories
and legends of Whitby and the
surrounding area as dictated by
Rex Greenwood circa 1999.

CHAPTER 1

There is excitement in the town as a wall has collapsed – probably due to the floods. Lately, there have been many changes. All manner of things has been happening, which is worrying. I must be wary of these changes. It seems strange what has occurred and how many visitors there have been. I have been playing Dracula for many years now; long before I came to Whitby. At least the 'Dracula Experience' is somewhere for me to rest for I need time. A lot more time. It's always the same, we never have enough time. Oh! But then I do?

Dance night comes around again. The Royal Hotel, my haven without fear. The one night when I can be myself – be Rex. Am I him. Or am I confused? Tonight, will give me the chance to clear my mind and be something different. But the call of the wild is always there!

"Now then Rex, are you in good form tonight?"

"Yes, Arthur, very good form." And I smile to

myself. Each Sunday I know someone will be dancing with a cut finger or a scratch on their hand. I note it, marking my time.

Now the 'dog' has gone, I hope I will be left in peace in my home of Whitby? I feel as if I have been in this place for many years. Wandering these old streets, looking for the old names.

'No, don't go back, you have acquired a new identity,' I tell myself. By day I am harmless, portraying Captain Cook of Whitby or causing much laughter as Count Dracula. People like the Count but only because they believe I will not harm them. If they only knew my real secret. What I have to do.

However, when I am finally done, I will need another new identity. When that time comes, I will know who or what I will be; I will know.

Yorkshire is in my blood and as the Count, the moors often call to me. In my journeys around them, I often encounter many ghosts or hear stories of untold mysteries which you can believe, or not. Either way, the choice is yours. Remember, ghosts seek you out. You don't seek them. Therefore, I know the power is mine. Ha! Ha! Ha!

Question: Do you believe in ghosts? If you do, dear friends, then why don't you join me. We can walk the roads surrounding Whitby to discover if such 'stuff' exists? You might be surprised by what you find. That is, of course, if you believe.

As I said, I often take trips to the North

Yorkshire Moors. It is handy for Dracula to meet all kinds of people. It also means I can maintain my blood bank! Although, I do have to put people at ease first as, unlike many of my predecessors, I don't want to rule by fear...

At the moment I will leave fear alone, although one day I may have to resort to it. Although I hope not. At least not until they come to destroy me. Other people, like the Professor[1], will come along with new ideas of destruction, but to no avail. They will not succeed.

The thought of fear takes me back to the Grosmont/Bog-Hall Junction Railway plate-layer[2]. Little do people realise I was the instigator of that little affair. One of the other workers plotted to harm the plate-layer, so I used his fear, hoping people would take note not to stray onto the railway lines for I would never be far away! Was he just another victim? Maybe!

Remember, if you venture to Grosmont, through the Bog-Hall tunnel to the sheds, you may hear a strange tap, tap, tap noise. It could be the headless man trying to find his way home. Or maybe me looking for another ghost lost to the living world – but not lost to me, as Dracula!

With the popularity of the Count having grown

---

[1] https://en.wikipedia.org/wiki/Abraham_Van_Helsing
[2] http://www.railwaysarchive.co.uk/documents/BoT_BogHallJunction1886.pdf

people often hold 'Dracula' themed dances or weekend breaks in and around the town. Perhaps one day I will arrange for them to have an exciting moment they won't quickly forget. There is to be such an event happening at Raven Hall. Now, where could you find another hall so conveniently situated with the right atmosphere which suits my haunting purpose? I have been photographed at the Hall, looking out to sea.

But that was before. I now know many ghosts are with me wherever I go for I often feel my 'life' is only just beginning. But no-one can understand the ordeal I experienced when I first met the Grey Lady of Raven Hall. Everyone who sees the Lady, or says they have the seen her, has a story to tell. Only I can assure you of the truth. Let me tell you about Raven Hall, the Grey Lady and my recent visit there...

Tonight, fear grips me, which is strange. An adversary of another kind never before experienced appears. Feline, wild, watching me as we dine in authentic surroundings. A cold feeling succumbs my body as my eyes are drawn to the nearby window. Like metal to a magnet. A grey cat, acute pointed ears and calculating, piercing eyes is watching me audaciously.

"May I get you some wine, Mr Greenwood?" the waiter asks, as he closes the curtains, bringing me out of a transfixed, hypnotic trance.

Dennis, a friend of many years, peruses the

wine list before ordering a sweet Barsac, stating it will complement the fish. In reality, I would prefer a deep red wine! More blood-like looking.

"Hello, surprise, surprise!" The lady of the hotel arrives. There is something about her face. Pretty and yet...? As people are introduced to one another, an uneasiness overcomes me. I feel the dominance of her stare. At times gentle, however with a knowing smile. Why do I feel fear? It is not normal for me. I close my eyes for a second, slightly shaking my head as if to rid myself of the feeling. Nonsense, I think to myself, enjoy the evening.

"Did you have a pleasant holiday, Pauline?" I make small talk. Despite my efforts, tonight I feel uncomfortable being with people. I have a sense of foreboding because of my past, although being dressed as Captain Cook helps me to adjust.

Dennis and his wife decide to take coffee in the lounge. Gwen, my wife, accompanies them. I make an excuse saying I need to take a short walk.

Outside it is dark. Not that darkness holds any fear for me; only restlessness. The grounds are a haven of walls, passages and out of the way gardens. One, in particular, intrigues me. It looks like an old disused altar waiting a sacrifice. I am yet to find my destination and my prey. I will see her. She knows I am here in the bright moonlight, cascading its light across the gardens, making each blade of grass shimmer different shades of green. The haunting stone altar looks inviting. Turning, I gaze out toward the calm, silent sea.

Suddenly I see a faint outline, a soft light colour. Pointed ears and a strange, almost soothing noise as though something is purring softly. Slowly, cautiously, I stretch my arm out trying to touch or catch my feline friend.

"Rex! What are you doing?"

"Pauline! I'm sorry. I didn't see you sat there. You startled me, do you often come out here at night? It seems rather chilly."

Composed, she appears to take charge. "I don't feel the cold very much now. I have become accustomed to living out here in the wilds! Do you feel the cold?"

I pause before answering. "No. Cold is my friend. I was looking for the cat. Your lovely wildcat." Later, I would learn there are two of them!

"Aren't you afraid of wild cats," she asks. "Especially at night? They are dangerous. Although you and your friend Dracula are experts of the night air, aren't you?" We both laugh a touch wickedly.

"Shall we wander back to the others?" she continues. "They are sure to have missed us." And turning she hesitantly walks away. No, 'walk' isn't the appropriate word. Pranced seems more suitable for she is the most beautiful animal of the species! A Cat!

The cold night is soon forgotten, the coffee

lovely and hot, the brandy superb. Feeling content and comfortable, I snuggle down into a large, soft, brown settee in the lounge. It has been a most enjoyable evening. My eyelids feel heavy. So heavy that I submit and close my eyes.

CHAPTER 2

The next thing I recall is Gwen shaking me awake. As I try to organise my disorientated mind, she calls across to some friends of Pauline's. They are a nice couple who want a photograph of me, knowing I play the parts of both Dracula and Captain Cook. I am only too willing to oblige as I love the recognition and the feeling of importance it gives me! The lady has severe arthritis. All I can suggest is garlic oil – good for arthritis, but bad for Dracula! I stifle a little chuckle at my own suggestion.

"My dear Dracula," the lady comments, "Your hand is bleeding; a small scratch."

I look at my hand astonished, and it appears I do have a small scratch, as if from a cat. But I didn't touch the cat – only Pauline, who scratched me lightly as we walked back to the hall. 'Must have been a branch you idiot,' I try convincing myself. 'What were you thinking?'

Pauline suggests I go into her office so she can clean it up but I decline the offer, implying I will lick and dab it clean with my handkerchief.

"No, I insist," she says dominantly, so reluctantly I follow her.

Alone in her office, she does the strangest thing. Showing intense, lustful pleasure she licks the fresh warm blood from my hand. Then she runs her tongue around her smooth, perfect, temptress lips; as if not wanting to miss a single drop. Still holding my hand, she looks up. Our eyes meet, and laughingly she cheekily says, "I feel like you now Dracula," and releasing my hand she turns and slips away.

Returning to the guests the elderly lady, still concerned, asks, "Let me see, has it stopped bleeding? Oh, yes, yes." And as I look, I see it has indeed stopped. There's not even a mark where the scratch had been. I feel somehow faint but beneficial.

She continues, "My boy, you did that well, no wonder you play Dracula so believably."

"Play Dracula! That's rich, very rich," interrupts Pauline almost cynically, glancing at my open hand and licking her lips provocatively. We all laugh but decide all good things must come to an end. It is time to leave. For me however, it is only the beginning.

As we depart the hotel, I notice the cat sitting on the reception desk. It is licking its lips. I see blood around its mouth. Perhaps it has caught a mouse? I hear it purring as if it's saying, 'Goodnight Dracula, meow.'

Outside, as I reach the hotel wall close to the swimming pool, I suddenly feel light-headed. "You go on ahead. I won't be long," I call out.

"Are you fine?" purrs a svelte cat-like figure as it passes from sight into the darkness.

I pause by the poolside. The metallic shine of the moonlight makes the water shimmer like tinsel on a Christmas tree. I feel like a naughty child daring to want to touch it. At this moment it appears so tempting and inviting. The breeze in the trees seems to be whispering to me. Have you ever sat by a poolside and felt the lapping sound of the water at the edge? Or heard the trees swaying and the grass whispering as it gently bends, creating a soft dirge of soothing, forgiving mindlessness.'

My mind is trapped in a lullaby of eerie sleep. If you ever feel tense, the noise of moving water is the most relaxing of sounds. I am fully relaxed, lying under the veranda of the outdoor pool, falling into a deep, deep satisfactory nothingness. Gently I slide into the pool, feeling no sensation of drowning. My hair floats around me, like an aquatic plant. My legs and arms do all the right things as I walk along the bottom of the pool with the lightness and dignity of a ballet dancer. It feels great! Wonderful! Don't ever break the spell, like Jonathan Livingston[*] – now that was an achievement of artistry when he flew for the first time!

There is a commotion. Suddenly my arms are grasped tightly, in a kind of awakening. I feel panic, there are many faces, and my lungs try to breathe in water. Water! That dreaded water. There is a taste of chlorine. I feel a spasm of pain in my chest. Something is pressing me hard, relaxing, then hard again, then relaxing. To me, it is all a blur. Finally, there is the tenderness of air into my lungs and warm breath, as if someone's lips are on mine, attempting to breathe oxygen into me. My chest heaves and all around there is a sense that they have won.

"Well done Pauline," I hear people say.

"Take him into the hotel and place him on the settee in my office."

All is quiet, and I fall into a deep, relaxing sleep. My friends and Gwen are reassured of my well-being.

Sometime later, I wake with no feeling of any ill effects. Strangely my clothes are dry. Making my way into the lounge I am ready to make, what I believe, will be a dramatic entrance. But I am greeted with, "Fancy fainting over a small scratch like that?"

Fainting? What about the pool commotion? Was I dreaming that?

"Now then Rex, fancy a brandy?" says Pauline, the perfect hostess, as always.

---

[*]https://en.wikipedia.org/wiki/Jonathan_Livingston_Seagull

Quietly I ask her, "Tell me, did I nearly drown?"

"Good Lord my friend, what makes you say that? You were washing the blood off your hand and must have fainted. You, silly boy, such a fuss."

I sit down feeling rather foolish and slightly confused. My friends are idly chatting, so my mind begins to wander.

In my mind, I am tracing back in time. Leaving Ruswarp Bank, going on to Scarborough Road then over the Iron Bridge at the river. It's a new crossing. More and more modernisation to the town. It appears the old mill is also extending and new houses are being built along the riverside. On to the mart where the cattle, sheep etc., are exchanged or sold, then uphill to meet the small roads off to Sleight and Littlebeck. I approach the road end where more minor roads lead down to Littlebeck, Falling Foss and Maybeck. Delightful areas, full of tranquillity and falling or running water. Woods of breath-taking colours, endless moors scattered with heather and sheep grazing obliviously; all are on view. Now I am at the main Scarborough Road, dipping and weaving where, along here, is the Boggle Hole turn off with many areas of interest. Then, on to the Falcon Inn for here is where I join the road to Ravenscar and Raven Hall, which is where I now am.

"Joanna, was I wandering?" I ask.

"Not surprising dear after your serious ordeal at the pool."

"You saw me?"

"Yes, the scratch on your hand, some ordeal, hey?"

Ever since meeting Pauline I have felt strange, and now Jo is in on the plot! Or, am I experiencing illusions. Only time will tell. I must be careful for I don't want to get caught out on some pretext or other. Just in case they know my secret and are friends of Hilda the Abbess. That is my one fear. That Saint Hilda's relatives, and friends will seek me out? Putting these thoughts behind me I know I will have to meet with Pauline again to discuss the Dracula themed week-ends she is planning at the Hall. A subject very close to my heart. Do I have one? A heart that is!

Finally, saying good-night we make our way across the car park to drive home and hopefully, to get a good night's sleep. But for me, it will be a time of reflection. Driving home all I can think about is the cat – the Raven Hall feline – curse her. Am I being unfair to the people at the Hall? But then I remember the history of the place, going back aeons ago, long before Roman times.

The many rituals of witch hunting that went on around the area. Maybe the wildcat has ancestors from those weird days. I must check for myself. The past! Have I found the Grey Lady or the legend of the same somehow? The cat – Pauline – the Grey Lady. Has my presence awakened a legend from long ago? I need to find out.

Question: Is it the cat, Pauline or the Grey Lady? Is the ghost of Raven Hall powerful? If so then Pauline must have the power of a wildcat to remind me of the Grey Lady.

But, does this also mean that Dracula is just an illusion when in the grounds of Raven Hall. No-one knows. No, only I as Dracula can experience the power. That feeling of night-dusk, the walls, the tunnel, the pool and the cliffs! Yet, in my adventures as Dracula, I still feel a little unsure, all because I hate water.

Life goes on and a few days later it is a normal rainy day in the life of the people of Whitby. Today the town is busy as the 150-year Railway Celebrations are happening. This also means there are more visitors, along with the mayors and dignitaries from around the area. John and Moira, two lovely people from the North Yorkshire Moors Railway, are liaising, having invited Gwen, my wife and myself to do the honours.

The Marchioness & Marquis of Normanby are at Whitby Station, the Viscount at Grosmont and Scarborough's Mayor at Goathland. There is bunting and flags everywhere along with commemoration plaques, etc. People are enjoying all the pomp as well as the lunches available in the Pullman Coaches.

Even as Captain Cook, I never forget nor run away from the fact that I must look for openings for my alternate ego, Dracula. After all, train doors are excellent places for causing damaged fingers. Blood can be smeared everywhere, meaning I will be rewarded.

And at last, I am.

"Goodness gracious Sir, let me look," I eagerly say to a young, pallid looking gentleman from the manpower services.

"Let me see. Oh yes, you have a small 'spell' in it," and before he can protest, I have his fingers at my eagerly, ready parted lips and I am biting gently but firmly to remove the small wooden splinter. His blood is warm and satisfying. Just enough for my palate; at least to make the craving disappear. "There sir, sorry about the dramatics but it is quicker this way. The pain should have gone now?"

"Why yes, Captain Cook, it has. Thank you," he says hesitantly, staring at me with a slight sneering smile. Little does he know. Or does he? Now he is under my spell. And, you never know, I might need him one day...

CHAPTER 3

Sunday morning is a beautiful part of the week, so I usually head for the church and the abbey. Both are standing prominently in magnificent splendour in the sunlight on the cliff above the old part of Whitby.

I pass Maggie's tea and sandwich bar situated on the edge of the abbey car park. She serves excellent refreshments, all at good value. "Hi, Maggie. Lovely Day."

"Coffee Rex, or should I say Dracula. Which part are you playing today?" She says this even though its obvious as I'm dressed as Dracula. After all, the day of the Sabbath shouldn't put me off performing.

"Now Maggie you will have your little joke. Coffee, please. Black, no sugar."

I listen as the wonderful bells of the old church ring out, "What a lovely sound. Calling the flock to confession. Sinners and Saints alike!" We both laugh.

"Err... excuse me, Sir, do you mind if I ask a few questions about the pirates' graves? Do you know where they are?" Turning, I see a short, stout, business looking man. Must be a tourist out for the day with his family. The children, two boys, aged about nine and ten, look bored and impatient. Apparently having no interest in the historical side of Whitby, even if it is about pirates. Nor it seems Dracula!

"But Dad, you said we could go to the amusements," the younger of the two brothers whines in a quiet but well-spoken, almost devilish voice.

"Later son. I said later," says the Father authoritatively before glancing back at me awaiting my reply.

"I don't mind at all," I tell him. "Let us take a walk to the church, so I can show you." And leading the way I explain further. "As you can imagine the line of stones is long. The ones with the skull and crossbones indicate the pirate's graves and are just as you enter from the Abbey Plain car park. On the right about 10-yards or so inside."

As we walk along, I tell him more. "Now Sir, legend has it, as it was told to me, there were two ships. One a merchant, the other pirate and both were off the coastline at the same time when an unfortunate encounter took place. It resulted in both ships being holed below the waterline. They were sinking fast. Many lives would have been lost but for two of the

46

pirates. They happened to be good swimmers, saving many men from both ships. However, when caught, the poor pirates were hung for piracy. So much for their bravery. Even so, they are buried in the churchyard, in consecrated ground." We stop and stare at the gravestones.

"A romantic legend or truth?" I ask the man. "Some say the pair can still be seen swimming, searching for survivors. Tell me Sir, have you any strange stories from your area?"

After a most interesting conversation with the man and his wife I eventually bid them farewell. Much to the delight of the children who have remained silent during our time together.

Turning to leave I pass Maggie on the way. She's a local Whitby girl, who relates to many things, such as the White Lady of the Abbey who it is said appears in the abbey windows at certain times. A lot of people say they have seen the White Lady. You see my friends, there are many tales and legends of Whitby and the surrounding area. And many more yet to be unfolded to me, as Dracula or Captain Cook.

"Bye Maggie, I must be on my way, as I have an appointment to keep." And, leaving the car park I venture down Green Lane, on to Church Street. Down past the old places where schools, chapels and houses once stood. Then down Grape Lane, past the Arches, over the bridge and across the Dockend car park.

Come my friends, let us continue our journey of

discovery into the legends and ghost stories of Whitby. There have been many changes: Stoker, Cook and now me. Yes. Even I have rung in some changes. Let me tell you of one.

The year was 1984. The month, October. It was at Bagdale Hall on the corner of Spring Hill. An excellent piece of old architecture the old Hall has long been associated with history. One of its oldest legends relates to a Captain Bushell who was reputed to be one of the first double spies. It seems he was quite fond of the ladies and lived at Bagdale Hall during the Cromwell era. As a Cavalier, he bade farewell to the maiden he loved, leaving the Hall to support the King. When he returned, he found the Roundheads were in occupation. They had hung or decapitated the young maiden. Capturing the Captain, unfortunately, the same fate befell him. Legend has it the Captain and his maiden still haunt the Hall to this very day, searching for each other. And, the room where the couple first met, always has an eerie feeling about it!

However, back to my story of 1984.

That night there was a party at which I was making an appearance as Dracula. The scene was set. Twenty-two young ladies from a shop in Redcar, a greengrocer I believe, were sat around a large round table in the Hall's lavish dining room. There was a large open fireplace. Its dog-grated splendour had the most beautifully decorated tiles inside a surrounding wooden cornice of ornate design. The dim lights of the chandeliers of icicles shone down from the low ceiling onto the Italian floor covering and the high-backed chairs.

I was to appear as Dracula at the low leaded windows, scratching on the glass to create hysterical screams of fright. I was also to rattle the outside door leading to the dining hall. Usually, it is kept locked but, as I touched the old metal door handle, the door suddenly burst open, flinging me violently and unexpectedly into the room. Off balance, I fell across the knee of the first girl sitting at the head of the table, who screamed uncontrollably. Even I was afraid! The door customarily barred and bolted, was this night, of all nights, open. The wind seemed to build up into a weird swirl. The candles and fire flickered harmoniously with our hearts, which were beating madly. I was aware we had awakened something. But what?

To this day, the girls still talk about that night.

Nor did it end there. After everyone had left, we were sat talking about the evening's events. Suddenly we heard a commotion coming from the kitchen. Making my way cautiously to investigate I was amazed to discover pots smashed on the floor and food strewn all over the walls! All I can say is, whoever or whatever it was, be it spirits, ghosts, poltergeists or living beings, even 'Dracula,' that night we all witnessed the disturbance. Whatever caused it, certainly made it very clear it wanted us out, and needed to be left alone to wander Bagdale Hall in peace.

Why don't you pause for a while, as I often do, while I recall something?

Many times, during the last three years as Town Crier extraordinaire, I have stood outside this magnificent building. Strangely I have also often heard the cries of long ago echoing along with my cries of 'Oyez, Oyez!' The battle cries, the screams of bloody wars, the clash of swords and the curses. Then peace. Yes peace, for I know they are watching us. But are they really at peace? I do wonder? Come let us move on.

Leaving Bagdale Hall, we will venture along Bagdale Road. Turning by Pannett Park up to Chubb Hill, on to Love Lane and down to Sandsend; the most beautiful tidiest little cove on the East Coast. It nestles in the valley just before Lythe Bank. Keeping on left of the valley, you come to the Fisherman's Cottages. I remember the day I was there in my official capacity as Town Crier...

"Oyez! Oyez! Oyez! Be it known this day that Sandsend has won an award for the tidiest village. A great and well-deserved honour."

The people of Sandsend are a jolly and happy community. More so today.

"Mr Greenwood, would you do me the honour Sir, of taking tea?"

"Caroline, how can one refuse such a lovely lady."

We enter a quaint, inviting cottage. There are two great stuffed pheasants with all their beautiful plumage, who seem to be looking at me, as if they know something! I decide to ask my hostess about the Old Fisherman. People say they've noticed him sitting in his rocking chair outside the house. Also, sometimes inside. I enquire if Caroline has ever seen him, but she says no. As we drink our tea, I get the occasional smell of strong pipe tobacco. Maybe it is my imagination. Bidding farewell to my hostess, I have a feeling there is someone else present. I still smell tobacco smoke! And I swear the stuffed pheasants' wink at me as I leave? Farewell Sandsend. Hold on to your dreams and stay tidy.

We are now back on the road progressing up Lythe Bank on past the churchyard to the magnificent church standing prominently and majestically, looking out to sea. Then, on to Lythe itself. If you approach Lythe Church at night from the north, you can see the light in the tower, searching outwards through the 'cross' opening; beckoning and inviting. It is told, that on a night when the moon is high and the cross aglow, the Lady of Lythe stands at the arch of the churchyard guiding motorists safely down the steep '1 in 4' gradient hill! Many a man has sobered up when seeing her, thus avoiding a serious accident! Good motoring Ladies and Gentlemen.

Half-way up Lythe Bank, we approach one of the many entrances to Mulgrave Castle, the home of the Marquis and Marchioness of Normanby. I have had the honour of presenting here at functions for the RAF stationed at Whitby and other such events. But, of the castle itself, I have talked to ex-maids who tell stories of ghosts. Especially of those wearing ball and chains. I am sure I will learn more of these, all in good time.

CHAPTER 4

Having lived in this romantic area for about seventeen years, I am in awe and wonder at the fables, legends and history of the villages. Such as Runswick Bay and Staithes which we are now approaching through Hinderland.

Mrs Cook, a dear friend, ran an excellent old-fashioned lodging house where I once lodged. With the sinking of the Potash mine (now complete) she had many miners from all over the world staying at her premises. Often our conversations would involve ghost stories from places not associated with Whitby such as Belgium, Poland, Germany and other European countries. Such a ghostly continent. But, also from other areas around our own great nation. One Irish gentleman, Mr Brogan, told us a story from when he was working in Barnburgh Main Colliery, in South Yorkshire.

They were sinking an air tunnel, from shaft A to B in order to change the flow of air, and were working in a drift of a '1 in 3' gradient. 'They' being the Brogans, Ganley's and Scots Mac. All men of incredible physique, although maybe not too bright but still, great guys to work with. The rock was very hard, being part of the 'park gate seam' and at a depth of about 2000 feet working conditions were very hot and dusty.

When the project started, the Ganley's opened up the tunnel to start the drift. But, one fateful night, while lowering the tubs down the incline, one tub broke away. Full of rock it careered into the work area. Poor Tom Ganley was the only one killed, just as he was about to tighten the bolts on the last archway to be put into position. Now normally the mine Blacksmith would have been doing this job using a standard spanner. However, on this occasion new bolts were being used, so a unique mover or ratchet spanner was called for. And Tom was using it.

After the accident, it was deemed too dangerous, so the area was sealed off. Five years later, it was reopened due to the air conditioning having to be improved lower down the drift for another deeper level. Having worked at Barnburgh Colliery, I can relate to why Mr Brogan came to be in the drift at the time. Bill had been using his own spanner but found he couldn't finish of the lock nut with it. About to look for the necessary ratchet spanner for the job someone, who he thought was a mate, handed it to him.

Finishing the job, he turned to say, "Right, let's go," only to discover no-one was there. Looking at the ratchet, he realised it was one no longer used. On the handle were the initials T.G. – those of Tom Ganley maybe! Or was it? To this day Bill believes his mates were pulling his leg, playing a joke on him. They, however, insisted they weren't working anywhere near him, saying none of them owned a spanner like that.

When the job was finally finished, it is said you could sometimes hear the sound of 'breaking away' the yell for runaway tubs. Were they all imagining it? No, for I believe, Tom will always be there.

Question my friends: What is real and what is fiction? How do you rate me? Well, I can assure you that even I wonder if I am me, if I really exist.

And now, onward to Grinkle Park and the mystery of the Lady of Grinkle or was it a monk?

We will go down Grinkle Lane which leads on and over to the main road, but let us pause first at the Grinkle Hotel. Mr Tennant – Michael to his friends, has the chair. He is a good, sound fellow, not prone to hysterics but, at this moment in time, he is pale, extremely pale.

"Come on Mick, tell me what is wrong. Perhaps I can help you? Is it ghostly?"

"At this time Rex, you must admit I am sober?"

"Well, yes. I would say so looking at you. Yes, very sober."

"Listen to me, Rex. To what I have recently experienced," and taking a deep breath he tells his tale. "I was cruising down Grinkle Park in my estate car with my brother. As we approached the gateway to the hotel, a hooded figure suddenly ran out. Right into the road. I couldn't avoid her; it was horrible. She bounced off the windscreen like a rag doll, rolling off lifeless. I know I drive fast, but safely. She didn't stand a chance," and he stops and pauses.

"She didn't stand a chance," he repeats. "I know I hit someone, or something? But, when I got out of the car, trembling with shock, I was horrified to see there was nothing there; no-one. I couldn't believe it. No scratch marks, no broken glass, nothing. Worst of all, was discovering there wasn't even... a body." And he shakes at the memory before finally saying, "My brother, still sat in the car, was shaken up but otherwise ok. I still can't believe it. We searched the area for a good half hour. But found nothing." And he sits back looking exhausted.

"Excuse me, did I hear you say you came down Grinkle Lane?" asked an old eccentric looking gentleman inquisitively.

Sitting up, Michael replied, "Yes, yes, why?"

"Well, my son, my name is Albert. I have lived around these parts for a long time. Perhaps I should tell you about an old story or legend. Many, many years ago Grinkle Lane was once an old coaching road for the mail. You will have heard of the likes of

Dick Turpin? And of course, how the post carriage had to get through at all costs. Not stopping for anyone, especially Highwaymen." And we nod our heads in agreement but remain silent.

"Well, one night the coach was tearing down the highway when the driver caught sight of a hooded figure crossing the road to Grinkle Hall. Too late, the coach couldn't stop in time. When it did, the coachman and guard jumped down, horrified and panic-stricken. They couldn't tell if the victim was a lady or a monk. Both men were filled with fear. But, more so with trepidation for the punishment they would receive if the mail didn't reach its destination on time.

"Together, in a form of frenzied terror and not really knowing what to do, they bundled the body up and took it into the wood. There they buried it in an unmarked grave beneath some bracken and moss before quickly leaving the area. Legend has it that the hooded figure is still looking for revenge for the loss of its life? Or maybe it's still trying to reach Grinkle Hall?" and here the man pauses before asking, "Tell me young man what do you think of legends and ghosts?"

As the man turns towards me, I sense him looking at me with eyes which are knowledgeable! I smile in return. The long, glistening tooth smile of Dracula. Poor old Albert never got another pint. And the lane, and its mystery, carries on to this day.

CHAPTER 5

Leaving Grinkle Hall, we will turn onto the main Guisborough Road heading for Commondale, Castleton. But first I must call and see Tom at the Cleveland Inn.

Entering the place, I greet him. "Hello, Tom."

"Well, upon my soul, come in, come in! These drinks are on me. What a surprise. Of course, I see you around Whitby ringing the news, but enough of that. You must have come for something. Sorry, that was inhospitable of me."

"No Tom, you are right. You see, I have been thinking about the first time I came up here. Do you remember? The bull's ring, hanging on a piece of twine from the hook in the wooden beam. Never did get the hang of that – costly though, very costly," and we both snigger at the memory. "No, what I came for Tom was to ask you about the haunting of

Commondale Moor?"*

A cold silent, deadly hush suddenly descends on the room. So silent I can hear the sizeable antique clock ticking away the time. What have I said?

"Look, my lad," says Tom rather irritably, "I like thee, and the missus, but forget Commondale and the Cleveland Pub for a while. Dracula, and Captain Cook tha' maybe, but it don't give thee the right, poetic or otherwise, to delve into our past. So, I say, Nay, good-day Mr Greenwood, see you sometime."

I leave wondering what Gwen will make of that. But I will be back soon enough. There is a legend here I am sure, and I want to know what it is. And I will find out about it. I will go back, and they will tell me what I want to know. They will have no option but to do so. Ha! Ha! Ha!

"Be prepared to defend yourself Tom." (I mean that for he is currently my fencing master.)

Leaving the moors road, we turn onto Castleton Road heading for Blakely Ridge, high up on the moors. It is a desolate place apart from the Lion Inn which, situated up on the ridge, is an inviting place for lonely tourists all year round.

Once inside the Inn, we will make the acquaintance of a small shepherd. His face is full of character, and I am drawn to ask him, "Have you been here long? Have you heard of the Lonely Shepherd of

_____

* Commondale Moor has a legend of a Black Dog

Blakely Ridge?"

"If you don't mind Sir," the landlord interrupts in a rather abrupt manner. "I would rather you both drink your beer quietly and leave the shepherd in peace."

Curiously I must ask, "Tell me, landlord, are you afraid of something... or someone? I don't suppose you have met me before. Ghosts are my fascination. My life is the afterlife, if you get my meaning."

"Oh, so you're the ghost hunter of Whitby. The one who plays Captain Cook and Dracula," he replies as he pushes his powerful chest out in my direction. "Perhaps you should be careful, for someday you might disturb the spirit world and then..."

I smile, slightly. "Then! Then what landlord? Do, to your knowledge, any ghosts haunt people? Ghosts are my friends and they are quite harmless. Only wanting to tell you their story. That is if you are willing to listen. Unfortunately, not many people have the time. Or they are too afraid to open their ears. But I'm not. Stories unfold you would never believe."

"Enough of that chat Mr Captain Cook," he responds in a loud authoritative voice, "I have more to do with my time than listen to your drivel."

After studying the man slightly, I say, "You do realise landlord, that something could suddenly happen in a moment and completely wipe you out. Your earthly life gone, in a flash. Unfinished.

Meaning you would then become the legend of Blakely Ridge. All because you had just disappeared and were unable to tell anyone. Unless of course, old Dracula, came along. Or your Lonely Shepherd. At least then we would know, wouldn't we? And we could write about you. The landlord who became famous in a ghost book of Yorkshire." I pause, letting my comments sink in. "So, now I have your attention landlord, we will happily finish our drinks and be on our way. Remember, it is your loss."

As we walk, I will tell you about my driving around the moors close to Fylingdales Early Warning Station. And how I discovered a road leading to Egton. Interesting, I thought, as it was here, I learnt that in 1600 there used to be a Catholic community. More a colony run by one of the priests, one Father Postgate. After 50 years of labouring in the settlement he was cruelly put to death in York, it was around 1619. His poor body being hung, drawn and quartered.

In 1857 Cardinal Wiseman opened the Catholic Church. It attracted a congregation from as far afield as twelve miles. No mean feat in those days as the moors-men of Egton were, to say the least, reluctant to even walk the roads over the moors, of which there are many. Roads, with no end in view at all, maybe only to the moors-men themselves. Recently, stories have begun unfolding about Father Postgate which I need to investigate further.

However, one legend is that a moors-man told how, after many years of walking across the moors, he lost his way one day. He ended up wandering, aimlessly over miles and miles of bracken and bog. Dirty, tired and with all hope gone he eventually lay down to die. And, as he did, he prayed. "Forgive me Father for no longer does my spirit rise to lead me from this dilemma, so I must die." Sleep soon overtook him as he waited for his fate. Now some will say the gasses from the bog made him sleepy and that he wandered in a stupor never to be seen again.

But to this day, the moors-man would tell you, that in his stupor he clearly saw Father Postgate slowly approach him. As if floating like a cloud. The Father then took the man firmly by the arm, and with head bowed, softly spoke. "Don't despair my son, we will walk the green together you and I, and will find our way."

And so, in a daze, yet not knowing how he managed it the moors-man hobbled on unsteadily. On through cloudy, tired eyes until finally he saw a familiar lane. Following it he arrived home safely, full of wonder and faith. Many times, people have been lost on the moors and, by some unknown hand, have been found or have wandered safely back home. Led by Father Postgate? Perhaps...?

Ha! Ha! I guess you are unbelievers. But I know. Oh, yes, I know. Acceptance is better than reason.

Yet sometimes, I even forget that I am Mr E. R. Greenwood. But, after all, what's in a name?

CHAPTER 6

Come we will make our way past Egton. It is here I recall once visiting a lady called Old Mary of Goathland. A farmhouse, looking very much lived in had come into view. To others it may have looked dilapidated and should perhaps have been pulled down. But to Old Mary it was her home. I had enquired at the farm for Mary, unaware it was where she lived. First time lucky you might say. Maybe not. Easy for my senses.

"Please, come in, Sir," Old Mary had said in a humble voice. "You wish to hear the story of the Lonely Shepherd, don't you? For anyone but you, I would be too afraid to tell the tale. Even for you I feel a sense of discomfort. Although I cannot say if what happened is truth or legend," and she pauses before continuing.

"Now, Thomas the Shepherd was out tending his sheep in November time. Dark came early that day. I remember the moon hadn't yet risen. Thomas was late returning. But, never as late as this. There are wild cats and foxes living on the moors which create detours for shepherds. But even so Thomas had never taken as long to return. The waiting seemed to never end. Of course, you don't go looking for a shepherd, for while you look, he could return home by another route. Four hours had elapsed. Nothing. All was quiet. You could feel a deathly silence."

Taking a breath, Old Mary shuddered as she recalled what happened next. "And then, there he was. I said, 'Good God, what the... Thomas!' But Thomas couldn't say anything. He just fell to the floor unconscious, like a lifeless doll. His clothing was tattered and covered in blood," and again she shudders before going on.

"After tending his open wounds, I sat by Thomas's side, waiting for him to come out of his exhausted state – hopefully with an explanation. How long he stayed in that uncontrollable sleep I do not know. My speculation as to what had happened was ripe and proved to be far from wrong. As I was to find out later to my amazement and disbelief. Yes, disbelief. At long last he opened his eyes and I tendered to his needs. Mainly of hunger, for little else did he require." Here she pauses yet again, staring as though in a hypnotic state.

"Good heavens Mary," I utter, rather excitedly, "don't keep me in suspense, tell me more."

She looks at me. "Be patient young Sir, for even

I haven't got long. Never the less I shall go on. Ye remember I said Thomas was well scratched and bloody. Well, what I am about to tell, you must keep to yourself as even I may suffer the wrath of evil that befell the wretched man," and she looked for my promise which I eagerly gave.

Then she continued. "Thomas, while looking for his lambs, discovered one was missing. He had never lost a lamb or sheep, except at birth. As such he was compelled to go in search of the animal. After what seemed an age to him, he sighted a movement in the valley of devils. The place so called due to the moans and strange sounds caused, many say, by the wind whistling around the large beaten rocks. Wild cats had also been seen roaming the moors during that year so one could not be sure. It was also said that the White Cat of Raven Hall had been observed. That is well known as being a devil cat." Old Mary looks at me questioningly, but I do not respond.

"Anyway, Thomas climbed down the cliff face some many feet, which is nothing for a shepherd, being all in a days' work. Before he reached the bottom a fiend suddenly sprang out, forcing him to fall. Its claws sank into different parts of his body. Thomas too terrified to make a sound, curled into a ball and covered his eyes with his arms. The beast repeatedly sank its fangs into his body, causing gaping wounds, which unfolded like an envelope. The excruciating pain became too much for him and, giving into despair and hopelessness, he felt his body go limp. He was ready to submit to his predator."

Old Mary stops speaking. She seems unwilling or unable to continue but after looking at me she swallows hard, takes a deep breath and goes on. "Suddenly, a screeching noise pierced his ears. He became aware of an indescribable presence and within seconds his oppressor had been transported into mid-air. Dazed, shocked and in severe pain Thomas passed out. Regaining consciousness his eyes tried to focus on what he thought was a giant black bird, watching him from a distance. Pulling his bleeding body upright, he leant against a flat rock, although he was still bent in two with pain. Rubbing his eyes, he tried again to recognise the type of bird. Was it an eagle? A falcon? He could not say. What he does remember was a chilling, shrieking sort of sound and then the words of… 'Go home Thomas. Tell no-one of this night. You are safe as long as you tell no-one.'"

Listening with intense interest I suddenly ask myself, 'Does Mary know? And if so how?'

"I know what you are thinking, Sir. But, as I have already told you I have not got long, so you will not see me again. Now, please go."

Many times, since that day I have enquired about Old Mary of Goathland, and Thomas the Lonely Shepherd. When I asked those in the area, the doors of Goathland would not open to me. I have also never found a grave for either Thomas or Old Mary. Goodbye Mary. I am sure we will meet again.

Question: Was this Legend or myth? You can never be sure. I think I know, but do you? Even I, who should never doubt myself, sometimes must. My only excuse is that I am still human! Or am I?

Branching off from Goathland we will go easterly, taking the first turn after the Grosmont junction road. Here you will see the lines of Shooting Butts, before eventually reaching larch woodlands, which are connected by a cart track to the moors. These gradually lead to Foss wood, then on to Falling Foss.

I stop walking, for now I think it is the time for us to part company. And so, I will take my farewell of you. You can go in peace and safety but, do not look back.

Vary your walk back to Whitby. Go via Littlebeck and then on to Sleights. Take the main road which runs through Sleights Village, passing over the bridge where the River Esk flows. If you are lucky you may see the ducks and their new born ducklings. The mothers are always watching, alert for any danger to their young. Turn at Salmon Leap, so called because this is the place where the Salmon battle against the sometimes, torrential, cascading waters forever trying to beat them back from returning to their homes. It is quite a tourist attraction when spawning time comes around. The instinct to return home is, I believe, built within us all. Follow the sign through Ruswarp then on to Whitby.

Goodbye dear friends and pleasant travels until we meet again. And we will believe me!

CHAPTER 7

Saying my adieus, I will leave my guests and depart. For some unknown reason, I am drawn towards the moor road leading over to Scarborough via Robin Hoods Bay. As I walk, I remember meeting Edna, who at that time lived in the valley bottom near Old Beck Tunnel. She used to tell me stories about the smugglers who crept through the old tunnels and along the roadways. Of the routes they used to get to the caves where they hid the spoils from the ships which sunk. All related in the 'Ward Lock and Company, Illustrations Guide of 1914-15.'

I also recall the time Edna told me a story of one such smuggler who, unfortunately fell to some cut-throats of the day. Taking a long time to die, he managed to crawl into the caves. Wailing and cursing with pain, he promised to return and avenge himself for their misdeed. It is said, if you stand on the slopes at Robin Hoods Bay, close to the old marine laboratory, you might hear him. On certain nights and even cold dreary days it is said the moaning seaman is heard searching for his tormentors. Or it could just be the wind blowing down the tunnel?

My head was lowered as I tried to conceal a pert grin, mutteringly disbelievingly, "Edna!"

"Oh yes," she replied sharply. "Besides, you of all people, surely don't believe in the wind 'theory,' do you?"

"Now, now Edna, you're putting words into my mouth," I say and lifting my head, after composing myself, there is a look of shocked hurt on my face. Then laughing, in a wicked sort of way I say, "Of course I don't believe, Edna."

That night I stay in Robin Hood's Bay at an old friend's house near the old beck which runs through Fylingthorpe. As night falls, I am found lying fully clothed on the bed, reminiscing about what Edna has told me. I have promised myself I will rise after midnight and go to listen for the moans. I am quite determined, but for once sleep overcomes me.

* * *

And so now, I must write the answer to all this.

How I remember the person I often meet in my dreams. Maybe this will be the last one. My Mother, Eva Ward, explains it all to me. Perhaps being the weakest at birth, being less than 2lbs or so, meant I needed more protection. It is only now that I realise, I was given it.

I consider my name, Eric Rex. But, what does

it mean. Let me tell you. Eric means good and kind; Rex means king and ruler. In all my life I have never knowingly or deliberately hurt anyone. The king and ruler, Rex, has had the power to look after himself. Strangely, the love I thought I had never been given when young, was there all the time. It is only now as time decreases that I have become aware of such things.

Since starting this book, I feel as if I have unlocked the capsule of time. The one we all have implanted deep within ourselves. I also see the future, the going forward which we all risk. In reality, the stories of ghosts I write about are not so much about ghosts but are of people who have gone before us. They too have been through that period of feeling unloved, before awakening to the real times of love in their life. All have experienced periods of hate and jealousy. Yet, we all have love and faith, of some kind.

No, I'm not unusual in the way I say or think these things. It is just an ordinary feeling of being needed, wanted, but mostly of being loved by the right people. To the aim of this explanation, let me say, I now realise, having played Dracula for so long, I understand what Mr Stoker was all about. He too was a weak child, yet he was showered with love. Remember, that word... 'love.' For, in reality, poor old Dracula was only the ghost of Stoker seeking love. We all have our own 'Dracula' within us. Our own secret dreams and desires, but still we all need love.

And so, as I end, bear in mind that anything that starts evil has to have had love at some time. And will, I hope, at some time return to that stronger feeling. I believe love is a powerful healer and we all have our own way of finding out or discovering a particular kind of love. Just, like Mr Stoker, his Dracula, his love...

By the way remember this:

Ghosts are as real or as ghastly as you wish them to be. But love is and could never, ever be considered a ghost. Nor, can it ever be considered that evil will go on forever.

It is our own kind of love that we must have. Maybe it just looks like evil?

IN RESPECT AND MEMORY OF
BRAM STOKER
FROM COUNT 'REX' DRACULA

ENTERTAINER WHO WAS AMBASSADOR FOR TOWN

TRIBUTES have been paid to a popular Whitby entertainer who raised thousands of pounds for charity. Rex Greenwood lost his 17-year battle with cancer on Sunday evening. The honorary citizen passed away in Whitby Hospital aged 78. Mr Greenwood was well known in Whitby from when he was the Town Crier, and often delighting children and visitors by dressing up as Captain Cook and Dracula. Mr Greenwood was born near Barnsley and when old enough started work in the mines where he worked his way up to being a 'winder-man.'

He moved to Whitby about 34 years ago with his wife Gwen. They ran the West Cliff Hotel and he worked for Cleveland Potash. Mr Greenwood enjoyed cycling and ballroom dancing and would often MC at dinner dances. But it was not until he moved to Whitby that he started to do a lot of charity work. He was the first person to give guided tours as Dracula and his interest in the character earned him a place on the BBC1 television series 'Noel Edmond's Telly Addicts.' He was even asked to go to Australia with his Captain Cook uniform as part of a special British week where he was adopted as the 'Captain Cook of Australia's Endeavour' replica ship. Over the years he has used his acting skills to raise thousands of pounds for Cystic Fibrosis, cancer charities and the James Cook University Hospital where he was treated.

He was one of the first people to be nominated as an honorary citizen of Whitby due to his charitable work. "He did a lot for charity and loved doing it," said Mrs Greenwood. He was Town Crier for eight-and-a-half years until his illness forced him to retire in 1989. "He put himself out a lot when he was Town Crier," said Mrs Greenwood. "He would go out at any time. If there was something to tell people he would be there."

He represented Whitby in various town crying championships. While many people knew him as the Town Crier, Dracula and Captain Cook, to his family he was a husband and a father. Married to Mrs Greenwood for 56 years they had two daughters. Mrs Greenwood's treasured memories of him include a trip to Venice just before their golden wedding anniversary. "It was absolute magic," she said.

Mr Greenwood's daughter Lynda said: "I remember the dad who sang us his songs and told us his stories at bedtime. He took us sledging and used to make swings and slides for us." His other daughter Mandy said: "He has always been there for us, even when we were young." Mr Greenwood also leaves behind grandchildren Grace, Daniel, Lisa and Ben.

Excerpt from Whitby Gazette, 04-10-2004